My Weird School Daze #2

Mr. Sunny Is Funny!

Dan Gutman

Pictures by
Jim Paillot

HarperCollins*Publishers*

To Emma

Mr. Sunny Is Funny!

Text copyright © 2008 by Dan Gutman

Illustrations copyright © 2008 by Jim Paillot

All rights reserved. Printed in the United States of America.

No part of this book may be used or reproduced in any manner whatsoever without written permission except in the case of brief quotations embodied in critical articles and reviews. For information address HarperCollins Children's Books, a division of HarperCollins Publishers, 10 East 53rd Street, New York, NY 10022.

www.harpercollinschildrens.com

Library of Congress Cataloging-in-Publication Data is available.

ISBN 978-0-06-134609-5 (pbk.) — ISBN 978-0-06-134610-1 (lib. bdg.)

Typography by Joel Tippie

13 LP/RRDH 10 9 8 7 6 5

First Edition

Contents

My name is A.J. and I hate school.

But I don't care about school anymore. You know why? Because last week I graduated from second grade at Ella Mentry School. And third grade doesn't start until September.

You know what that means?

That's right! It's summertime! I don't have to worry about school for THREE WHOLE MONTHS!

Yippee!!

Before school ended my teacher, Mrs. Daisy, told us to write about our favorite season. We had to read our essays in front of everybody.

"My favorite season is spring," wrote Andrea Young, this annoying girl with curly brown hair. "The sun is out. Flowers are blooming. Birds are chirping. Butterflies flit to and fro. It fills me with joy and happiness."

I hate Andrea.

What is her problem? Everybody knows the best season of all is summer. That's the first rule of being a kid! Summer blows the doors off the other seasons.

You know why summer is so great? Because you don't have to sit still all day. You don't have to pledge the allegiance or have circle time or learn the Word of the Day. You don't have to line up in ABC order and walk in single file. Teachers don't yell at you, and you can't be sent to the principal's office. There's no disgusting cafeteria food to eat. You don't have to read books. No homework! You don't have to learn stuff.

My brain hurts from so much thinking all year long. In second grade I thought my head was gonna explode from thinking too much.

During the school year, you have to go to bed early and get up early. In the summer you can stay up late and get up late. The sun stays out until nine o'clock at night. How does it know to do that? I guess the sun likes summer, too.

Summer is like three months of recess! You can have water balloon fights, eat saltwater taffy, and play football on the beach. And you don't have to wear a coat or gloves. You can wear flip-flops and shorts with holes in them. Ice cream tastes better. And you don't have to take as many showers because you can go swimming. I love swimming. I'm a great swimmer. In the summer you can swim all day.

Plus, in the summer when you get sunburned, you can peel off your skin!

What's cooler than peeling off your own skin?

But here's the number one reason why summer is the best season: I don't have to see Andrea Young for THREE WHOLE MONTHS!

Yippee!!

Three months is 12 weeks. That's 12 whole weeks with no Andrea!

I got a calculator for Christmas, and I figured it out. Twelve weeks times 7 days in a week is 84 days.

That's 84 days with no Andrea!

And 84 days times 24 hours in a day is 2,016 hours.

That's 2,016 hours with no Andrea!

And 2,016 hours times 60 minutes in an hour is 120,960 minutes.

That's 120,960 minutes with no Andrea!

And 120,960 minutes times 60 seconds in a minute is 7,257,600 seconds.*

---

*Aren't calculators cool?

That's more than 7 million seconds with no Andrea!

Yippee!!

And I'm going to enjoy every one of them.

Hitting the Beach

This summer, my parents rented a beach house. We were gonna share it with my cousins, but they couldn't come. So we'll have a big beach house all to ourselves!

The day after school ended, we packed up the car and drove a million hundred miles to the ocean.

"I can't wait to hit the beach," I said, looking out the car window.

I had to sit in the back with my sister, Amy, who is going into sixth grade. She's annoying, but not as annoying as Andrea.

"You'd better watch out for the sand monster, A.J.," my sister said.

Sand monster? I never heard of a sand monster.

"There's no such thing as a sand monster," I said.

"Oh, yes there is," Amy told me. "He's a zombie who lives under the sand. He comes out when you least expect it. And he only eats boys."

I bet Amy was yanking my chain. But I

decided to keep my eyes open for man-eating zombie sand monsters just to be on the safe side.

We stopped at a Chinese restaurant

because there wasn't any food at the beach house. Chinese food is cool because they give you chopsticks. So while you're waiting for the slowpoke grown-ups to finish eating, you can drum on the table or put the chopsticks in your nose and pretend to be a walrus.

Finally, we reached the beach house. It was too late to go swimming, but my parents said I could check out the beach while they unpacked our stuff.

The ocean smelled good. There was a sign on the boardwalk that said SAND CASTLE CONTEST THIS WEEK. Up in the sky, somebody was parasailing. Do you know what parasailing is? A parachute is strapped to your back, and a boat pulls you with a rope. Parasailing is cool. I'm gonna try it when I get bigger.

The beach was almost empty, except for one thing—a backhoe. Do you know what a backhoe is? It's this yellow machine that digs up stuff.

The backhoe was scooping up sand and dumping it onto a big pile. I went over to watch because machines are cool.

A teenager was driving the backhoe. He had blond hair and a whistle around his neck.

"Yo, dude!" he said as he turned off the motor. "My name is Evan, but everybody calls me Mr. Sunny. What's your name?"

"My name is Arlo, but everybody calls me A.J.," I said. "What are you doing?"

"Building a sand castle," Mr. Sunny said. "I'm gonna enter the contest."

"It looks like a big pile of sand to me."

"Oh, wait until it's done, man," Mr. Sunny said. "Right now my castle is hidden within this sand, waiting to be born. Sand is my life, dude."

Guys who say "man" and "dude" are cool. Mr. Sunny seemed pretty nice, even if he did like sand a little too much.

"Is this your summer job?" I asked. "You build sand castles?"

"No, dude," Mr. Sunny said. "I'm the lifeguard here. Will I see you out in the water tomorrow?"

"You bet!" I said. "I'm a great swimmer."

It was getting late. I said good-bye to Mr. Sunny and headed back to the beach house.

"I have great news, A.J.!" my mom yelled from the porch. "I just got off the phone. One of your friends from school is going to be sharing the house with us!"

"Yippee!" I said. "Who is it? Ryan? Michael? Neil?"

"No," my mother replied. "It's Andrea Young."

WHAT?????????!!!!!!!!!!!

Bummer in the Summer!

Noooooooooooooooo!

Not Andrea! Why did it have to be Andrea? Anybody but Andrea! Weren't there any bank robbers or criminals we could share our beach house with?

Little Miss Perfect Know-It-All is so annoying. She thinks she is really smart. I know she'll be hanging around me all summer, bothering me, and trying to show off how much she knows about everything.

"Please don't let Andrea come here!" I begged my parents. "Please please please please?"

Saying the word "please" over and over again will usually make grown-ups give you anything you want. Nobody knows why.

But it didn't work this time.

"A.J., you be nice to Andrea," my mother told me. "Her mother and I are good friends."

I don't get it. Why do I have to be

friends with somebody just because her mom and my mom are friends? It's not fair.

The next morning a car pulled into the driveway, and guess who got out?

Little Miss Annoying and her parents! Andrea was wearing pink sunglasses and a bathing suit that had butterflies on it.

"Hi, Arlo!" said Andrea, who calls me by my real name because she knows I don't like it. "Isn't this going to be

a great summer?"

"It *was* gonna be a great summer," I said, "but then you showed up."

"That's not nice, Arlo!"

"Neither is your face," I told Andrea.

My mother told me to be a gentleman and carry Andrea's suitcase upstairs for her.

"What do you have in here, rocks?" I asked.

"No, silly," Andrea said. "Books! It's my summer reading. Every summer I set a goal for myself. This year my goal is to read the complete works of Shakespeare."

"You're gonna read about a guy who shakes a spear?" I asked.

"William Shakespeare is the most famous writer in history!" Andrea said. "If you opened a book once in a while, you'd know that, Arlo."

"Hey, I opened a book once," I said. "And then I closed it."

"Why?" she asked.

"Because there were words inside."

Andrea picked up one of her dumb Shakespeare books and started reading out loud:

> "*To be, or not to be, that is the question:*
> *Whether 'tis nobler in the mind*
> *to suffer*

The slings and arrows of outrageous
*   fortune,*
Or to take arms against a sea of
*   troubles*
And by opposing end them.'"

"Isn't that lovely, Arlo?" Andrea asked.

"*Zzzzzzzzz,*" I said, pretending to be asleep.

That Shakespeare guy made no sense at all. The question isn't to be or not to be. I'll tell you what the question is. Do you want ice cream or cake? That is the question. Trick biking or skateboarding? That is the question. TV or video games? That is the question. Would it be better if a piano or an elephant fell on Andrea's head? That is the question.

Andrea lined up her dumb books on a shelf in ABC order.

"Hey, maybe we can read together on the beach, Arlo!" Andrea said. "What did you bring for summer reading?"

Summer reading?! What is her problem? "Summer" and "reading" are two words that should never be put together in the same sentence. The only reading I brought was a comic book that I finished in the car. It was about a superhero named Mold Man who can turn his body into any shape. He's cool. I bet Mold Man would kick

Shakespeare's butt.

Andrea's mom said we could go to the beach as long as we came back in time for lunch. Then we'd have to wait an hour before we went swimming again. Mothers always make you wait an hour after you eat before you can go swimming. Nobody knows why. I guess sharks can smell the food in your stomach and will eat you to get it.

I showed Andrea how to get to the beach. The backhoe was gone, but Mr. Sunny was out there working on his big pile of sand. He was concentrating so hard that he didn't even notice us.

"Who's that boy?" Andrea asked.

"That's Mr. Sunny, the lifeguard," I told her.

"He's a hunk!" Andrea whispered.

"A hunk of what?" I asked.

"He's dreamy!"

Andrea had on a zombie face. Her mouth was open, and she was making goo-goo eyes at Mr. Sunny.

Ugh, disgusting!*

---

*Enjoying the story so far? Good. So what are you reading this for? The story's up there, dumbhead!

Mr. Sunny Is Weird

Mr. Sunny had a baseball cap on his head and earphones in his ears. He was working very hard on his sand castle, using a plastic shovel to carve the walls. Finally, he noticed me and Andrea watching him.

"Hi, A.J.!" he said. "Who's your girl-friend?"

"She's not my girlfriend," I said.

"I'm not his girlfriend," Andrea said.

"Well, who's your friend that's a girl?" asked Mr. Sunny.

"She's not my friend, either," I told him. "Friends are people you like. This is Andrea."

"Charmed," Andrea said, all giggly. She did one of those courtesy things girls do. "I love your sand castle!"

What a brownnoser! As soon as Andrea started talking to Mr. Sunny, she acted like I wasn't even there.

"I'm gonna win the contest," Mr. Sunny said. "First prize is a trip to France. I'm gonna go to college there and study sand sculpture from the great sand masters."

"That sounds awesome," Andrea gushed. "Are you in high school?"

"Yeah, I'm sixteen. "

"Is Sunny your real name?" asked Andrea.

"Nah," Mr. Sunny said. "My name is Evan. Everybody calls me Mr. Sunny because I love the sun so much."

"'What's in a name?'" said Andrea. "'That which we call a rose by any other name would smell as sweet.' Shakespeare wrote that, you know."

Ugh.

Mr. Sunny took off his baseball cap and showed it to us. It had solar panels built right into it! Then he turned around and showed us that his tank top had solar panels built into it too.

"The solar panels power my iPod," Mr. Sunny told us. "Why do we have to burn gas or coal when all the power we need is right there in the sky? Global warming is a bummer, man."

"I hate global warming," Little Miss Brownnoser said. If Mr. Sunny said he hated butterflies, Andrea would probably say she hates them too.

"Excuse me," Mr. Sunny said. "I can't talk right now. I have to work on my sand castle before the beach fills with kids."

" 'Men of few words are the best men,' "

Andrea said. "Shakespeare wrote that too."

Mr. Sunny took off his shirt and went back to carving the castle. When he turned around, I could see the word "SUNNY" written across his back in white letters.

"Is that a tattoo?" I asked.

"No," Mr. Sunny said. "I cut the letters *S-U-N-N-Y* out of paper and taped them to my back. It's a SUNNY sunburn!"

Andrea was all giggly and told him his sunburn was cool.

"I bet you have lots of girlfriends," Andrea said.

"Oh, I don't have time for that," Mr. Sunny replied. "Sand is my life."

Mr. Sunny is funny! But if you ask me, people who wear solar panels and tape letters to their backs are weird.

Soon the beach was filled with people, blankets, and umbrellas. I went for a swim. When I came back, Andrea and a bunch of other kids were gathered around Mr. Sunny.

"Part of being a lifeguard is to teach you kids about first aid," he said. "Does anybody know what to do if a person is drowning and can't breathe?"

Little Miss I-Know-Everything waved her hand in the air, just like she was at school. But Mr. Sunny called on me. So nah-nah-nah boo-boo on Andrea.

"It depends on who's drowning," I said. "If the quarterback of your Pee Wee football team is drowning, then you have to get a new quarterback right away. Because if you don't have a quarterback, you'll have to forfeit the game."

Everybody laughed even though I didn't say anything funny. Andrea rolled her eyes.

"How about you, Andrea?" asked Mr. Sunny.

"If somebody is drowning," she said, "you give them mouth-to-mouth resuscitation."

"That's right!" Mr. Sunny said.

Andrea stuck her tongue out at me. I

stuck mine out right back at her.

"Arlo, don't you remember when Officer Spence gave mouth-to-mouth resuscitation to Mrs. Daisy at our graduation?" Andrea asked. "It was just last week!"

How am I supposed to remember what happened last week?

"Do you need a volunteer to practice mouth-to-mouth resuscitation on?" asked one of the girls. They all got giggly and waved their hands in the air.

"Me! Me! Me!" shouted Andrea. "Please please please please pick me!"

"Okay," Mr. Sunny said. "Andrea, you're my volunteer."

"Yay!" Andrea squealed, jumping up

and down. I tell you, that "please" thing works every time.

Mr. Sunny told Andrea to lie on the sand.

"Okay," he said, "pretend you were drowning. I dragged you up on the beach, and you can't breathe."

"I can do that," I said.

"You can pretend you were drowning and you can't breathe?" Mr. Sunny asked.

"No, I can pretend that Andrea was drowning and can't breathe," I told him. "I do it every day."

"You're mean, Arlo!"

Mr. Sunny knelt down next to Andrea. She closed her eyes.

He tilted her head back a little and

pinched her nostrils shut with his fingers.

Then he told us he was going to pretend to blow a few breaths of air into Andrea's mouth so she would be able to breathe again.

He leaned over until his mouth was almost touching hers.

Andrea puckered up her lips.

Ew, disgusting! Mr. Sunny was about to kiss Andrea! I thought I was gonna throw up.

That's when the strangest thing in the history of the world happened.

"Shark!" somebody yelled. "There's a shark in the water!"

A Strange Visitor

We all looked up. Sure enough, in the distance there was a shark fin sticking out of the water!

"WOW!" everybody said, which is "MOM" upside down.

"Eeeeeeeeeeeek!" somebody screamed.

Sharks are scary! My friend Billy, who

lives around the corner, told me a shark can bite your head off like it's eating grapes. I saw a movie where this shark ate a bunch of people. In the end some guy threw a tank filled with gas in the shark's mouth and blew it up. It was cool.

Everybody on the beach was yelling and screaming and freaking out. You

should have been there!

Mr. Sunny blew his whistle and shouted, "Everybody out of the water! Leave this to me. I know how to handle sharks. I'll lure it away from the beach."

Then he went running into the ocean.

"Mr. Sunny is sooooooo brave!" Andrea sighed.

"That's not brave," I said. "That's dumb. The shark could bite his head off like a grape."

We all watched as Mr. Sunny dived into the water. He was swimming right toward the shark! What a dumbhead!

I was sure the shark was going to bite Mr. Sunny's head off like a grape. But it

didn't. Because just as Mr. Sunny reached the shark, we figured something out.

It wasn't a shark after all!

No, it was a guy with a shark fin strapped to his back!

Mr. Sunny dragged him up onto the beach. The guy was wearing flippers and a diving mask. We all gathered around. I thought Mr. Sunny might have to give the guy mouth-to-mouth

resuscitation. He was choking and spit-
ting out water.

"Glub, glub," said the guy.

"Are you okay, dude?" asked Mr. Sunny.

"G'day, mates!" the guy said. He had a
funny voice. "Yes, I believe I am okay."

"What's your name, man?" asked Mr.
Sunny.

"George Granite."

"Dude, why do you have a shark fin
attached to your back?" Mr. Sunny asked.
"You scared us to death, man!"

"I am a long-distance swimmer," Mr.
Granite said. "Sometimes I roll over on
my back, and the fin helps me stay in a
straight line."

"Where did you swim from?" somebody asked.

"Australia."

WHAT???!!!

"Australia?!" I said. "That's like a million hundred miles away!"

"You swam all the way across the Pacific Ocean?" asked Andrea.

"Well, I did stop to rest on a passing turtle," Mr. Granite said.

It was totally amazing. But if you ask me, people who swim across oceans with shark fins on their backs are weird.

Nah-Nah-Nah Boo-Boo

Y'know how your teacher says you have to read a chapter in a book before you can have fun? And you really don't want to? Well, read this chapter. Then go have fun! And tell your teacher nah-nah-nah boo-boo!*

---

*Made you look down!

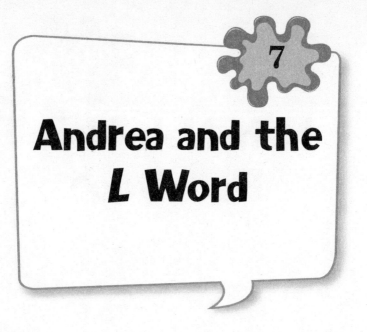

Andrea and the *L Word*

Great news! The next day, my parents said my friends Ryan and Michael and Neil could come and spend a week with us at our beach house. Yay! I guess my parents felt bad about sticking me with Andrea all summer.

I was so excited when Michael's dad

pulled his car into the driveway. Me and the guys went right out to the beach to play football. Our Pee Wee football team lost every game last year. But we are getting a new coach this year named Coach Hyatt. So maybe we'll be better.

"Go out for a long bomb!" I shouted to Ryan.

Playing football in the sand is cool because you can dive for the ball like they do on TV. And when you're all hot and sweaty, you can just jump into the water to cool off.

When me and the guys got tired of playing football, we walked down the beach. Mr. Sunny was working on his

sand castle. He had rulers, buckets of water, Popsicle sticks, and lots of other carving tools. And guess what brown-nosing know-it-all was helping him?

Andrea, of course.

"Hi, Mr. Sunny!" I said. "These are my friends Ryan, Michael, and Neil. We call Neil 'the nude kid' even though he wears clothes."

"I'm sorry, Arlo," Andrea told me, "but Mr. Sunny cannot talk to you right now. He is a sand artist."

Except that she said "arteest." What's up with that?

"The sand is my canvas," Mr. Sunny said without even looking at us.

"The sand is Mr. Sunny's canvas," repeated Andrea.

"I must have just the perfect mixture of sand and water to create my sand masterpiece," said Mr. Sunny. "I call it my sanderpiece."

"Mr. Sunny must have just the perfect mixture of sand and water to create his sanderpiece," repeated Andrea.

"I am one with the sand," said Mr. Sunny. "The sand speaks to me."

"Shhhhh!" said Andrea. "Mr. Sunny is speaking with the sand."

Mr. Sunny closed his eyes and was mumbling something to himself. I couldn't hear all the words, but it had something to do with sand.

Sheesh! People who talk to sand are weird.

Andrea stepped away from the castle and pulled me aside.

"Arlo, I'm in *love*!" she whispered.

Ugh! Andrea spoke the *L* word!

"With who?" I asked. "Besides yourself, I mean."

"Who do you think?" Andrea said. "Mr. Sunny! He's brave and handsome, and he's an artistic genius! See how he leans his cheek on his hand? 'O that I were a glove upon that hand, that I might touch that cheek!' Shakespeare wrote that, you know."

Oh, brother! That Shakespeare dude was annoying.

The guys came over to hear what Andrea was whispering about.

"Mr. Sunny is sixteen years old," I told Andrea. "He's way too old for you."

"I already figured it out," Andrea said. "Mr. Sunny is seven years older than me. So when he's thirty, I'll be twenty-three. That's not so bad. And when he's fifty-eight, I'll be fifty-one. And when he's—"

"Okay, I get it," I said. "But he's too old for you now."

"I don't care," Andrea said. "'Love is blind, and lovers cannot see. The course of true love never did run smooth.'

Shakespeare wrote that too."

"Did that guy ever write anything in English?" I asked.

"Shakespeare *was* English, you fobbing, toad-spotted, maggot pie!" said Andrea.

"Oh, snap!" said Ryan.

"Are you gonna take that, A.J.?" Michael said. "She called you a fobbing, toad-spotted, maggot pie."

"I don't even know what that means," I said. "It's in that Shakespeare language."

"It sounds like bad words to me," said Neil the nude kid.

"I have it all planned out," Andrea told us. "When I grow up, Mr. Sunny and I will be married right here on the beach. We'll have a solar-powered bungalow and cook our meals on a solar-powered stove. I'll help him build sand castles all day long. It will be *sooooooo* romantic."

"Does Mr. Sunny know about this?" asked Ryan.

"Oh no, " Andrea whispered. "It's a secret. I'm not going to tell him until I'm eighteen and he's twenty-five."

Girls are weird.

Love Is Dumb

"Girls are weird," I told the guys as we walked away from Andrea.

"You can say that again," Michael said.

"Girls are weird."

We walked down the beach to scope out some of the other sand castles that people were building. They were really lame.

"Girls are always falling in love," Ryan said.

"Ugh, disgusting!" we all agreed.

"I'm never gonna fall in love," said Neil the nude kid.

"Me neither," said Michael. "Love is dumb."

"Well, if Andrea is in love with Mr. Sunny, at least she won't be bugging *me* anymore," I told the guys.

"I think you're jealous, A.J.," said Ryan.

"What?!"

"You're jealous that Andrea's in love with Mr. Sunny."

"I am not!" I insisted.

"Are too," Ryan said. "You tried to talk her out of being in love with him."

"I did not."

"Did too."

We went back and forth like that for a while.

"Oh, come on, A.J.!" said Michael. "It's so obvious you and Andrea are secretly in love. That's why you're so mean to each other. Everybody knows that if you like a girl, you act like you hate her."

What? That didn't make any sense.

"Yeah," Neil said, "if you really hated Andrea, you would act nice to her. That would prove that you hate her."

My brain hurt.

We went up on the boardwalk and bought saltwater taffy with some money my mom gave us. I got a bag of chocolate taffy. Michael got cinnamon taffy. Neil got strawberry taffy. Ryan got broccoli taffy. Ryan will eat anything, even stuff that isn't food. One time he ate part of the seat cushion on the school bus.

I thought about what the guys said. Being mean to Andrea showed that I liked her. And being nice would show that I hated her. So if I wanted the guys to stop teasing me about being in love with Andrea, I would have to be really nice to her.

We went back down to the beach to see how Mr. Sunny was doing on his castle. He was talking to the sand with his eyes closed. I called Andrea over.

"I bought you a present," I said, handing her my bag of saltwater taffy. "Sweets to the sweet."

"Oh, thank you, Arlo!" Andrea said. "I didn't know you knew Shakespeare!"

"Huh?"

"'Sweets to the sweet,'" she said. "Shakespeare wrote that."

"He did?"

"Oooooh!" Ryan said. "A.J. is talking that Shakespeare talk to Andrea and giving her candy. They must be in love!"

"When are you gonna get married?" asked Michael.

If those guys weren't my best friends, I would hate them.

Much Ado About Nothing

Me and the guys went back up to the boardwalk. We walked past a Chinese fast-food restaurant there. Just seeing it made me hungry. But I couldn't get food because I spent the money my mom gave me on saltwater taffy. And I gave most of the taffy to Andrea.

Bummer in the summer!

"What do you wanna do?" I asked the guys.

"I don't know," said Ryan. "What do you wanna do?"

"I don't know," said Michael. "What do you wanna do?"

"I asked you first," I said.

We went back and forth like that for a while. Finally, Neil the nude kid suggested we go booger boarding, which made no sense to me. Who wants to put boogers on a board? But then he said he meant *boogie* boarding, which is completely different and much more fun.

The only problem was that we didn't

have a boogie board.

"We could dig a hole," suggested Ryan.

"Digging holes is cool," said Michael.

"Maybe we'll find buried treasure," Neil the nude kid said. "Then we can use it to buy some food."

We went down to the beach to dig a hole. My friend Billy, who lives around the corner, told me that if you dig a hole deep enough, it will go all the way to China.

"Hey," I told the guys, "if we dig a hole to China, maybe we'll end up near a Chinese restaurant. I bet they'll give us Chinese food."

"Then we won't even need to find buried treasure," Michael said.

"Great idea, A.J.!" said Ryan.

That's why I'm in the gifted and talented program at school.

The four of us started digging with our hands. I could almost taste the Chinese food we were going to eat once we reached China.

"Hey," Ryan said, "what's the deal with jumbo shrimp? It's either jumbo or it's shrimpy. It can't be both."

"Yeah," said Michael, "and how can you have sweet and sour pork? Either it's sweet or it's sour. What's up with that?"

"Yeah," I said, "and how do they know which ribs are the spare ones?"

Chinese food is weird.

We were all digging in the sand when the strangest thing in the history of the world happened.

"Hey!" Neil suddenly shouted. "There's something down here!"

"What is it?" I asked. "Buried treasure?"

"No, it's . . . a hand!"

"Ahhhhhhhhhhhhhhhhhhhhhh!" we all screamed.

"And the fingers are moving!"

"Ahhhhhhhhhhhhhhhhhhhhhh!" we all screamed.

"It's the sand monster!" I shouted. "My sister told me about it. It's a zombie, and it eats boys!"

"Run for your lives!" shouted Neil.

That's when this giant, human-shaped creature pushed its way out from under the sand.

It stood up!

"Ahhhhhhhhhhhhhhhhhhhhh!" we all screamed.

The sand monster started shaking sand off itself.

And that's when I realized it wasn't a sand monster at all. It was Mr. Granite, that weird guy who swam all the way from Australia!

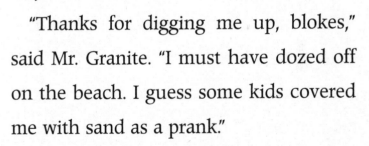

"Thanks for digging me up, blokes," said Mr. Granite. "I must have dozed off on the beach. I guess some kids covered me with sand as a prank."

Then he just walked away, like that was completely normal. Mr. Granite sure has a weird way of popping up out of nowhere.

Down the beach, we saw that Mr. Sunny had put up a big fence around his sand castle. I guess he was afraid that somebody might damage it before the judging. A bunch of kids were watching him work on the castle, but Andrea wasn't around.

"Where's Andrea?" I asked Mr. Sunny.

"I cannot talk right now," he replied. "I must have silence with the sand."

We found Andrea down by the water, reading one of her Shakespeare books.

She looked like she had been crying.

"What's your problem?" I asked Andrea.

"Mr. Sunny won't talk to me," she said, dabbing her eyes with a tissue. "He always says he needs to be alone with his sand. 'These words are razors to my wounded heart'! 'This was the unkindest cut of all.' 'O, I am fortune's fool'! 'Alas, I am a woman friendless, hopeless'!"

That Shakespeare talk is really annoying. But I never saw Andrea cry before. I almost felt sorry for her. Almost.

That's when I got the greatest idea in the history of the world. I could prove once and for all that I didn't like Andrea.

"I know how you can get Mr. Sunny to notice you," I told Andrea. "You should pretend to drown. Mr. Sunny will have to save you."

The guys all agreed that I was a genius, and I should get the No Bell Prize. That's a prize they give out to people who don't have bells.

"It would never work," Andrea said. "I've been taking swimming lessons since I was three. I'm an excellent swimmer."

"Mr. Sunny doesn't know that," I told her. "Just fake it and pretend you can't swim."

"But that would be like lying," Andrea said.

Andrea doesn't know the first thing about lying. Lying is when you say your dog ate your homework when you don't even have a dog.

"Pretending to drown isn't lying," I told her. "You can't tell a lie if you don't talk. And if you're drowning, you don't talk. Except to yell 'Help!'"

"Actually, drowning people say 'Glub, glub,'" said Michael. "I saw that in a movie once."

"First they yell 'Help,'" Ryan said, "and then they say 'Glub, glub' as they're drowning."

"I don't care what drowning people say!" Andrea yelled. "I won't do it!"

Sheeesh, what a grouch.

The Sanderpiece

The next morning me and the guys saw a sign on the boardwalk that said SAND CASTLE JUDGING TODAY! It said that a judge would be coming down the beach to choose the best sand castle. The winner would get a trip to France.

"Hey, what's that?" Neil asked, pointing up at the sky.

"Somebody is parasailing," I said, and I told the guys what parasailing was.

"That is cool!" they all agreed.

We went down to the beach. A bunch of kids were looking at Mr. Sunny's sand castle through the fence. It was amazing. It looked just like a real castle.

"I must have silence as I put the finishing touches on my sanderpiece," Mr. Sunny said. "It must be perfect so I can win the trip to France."

Mr. Sunny had hooked up an electric toothbrush to his solar-powered baseball cap. He was crawling around on the

ground, using the toothbrush to brush away the last tiny specks of loose sand.

"Your sand castle rocks, Mr. Sunny!" Michael said.

"It's gonna blow the doors off all those other sand castles," I told him. "You're sure to win the contest."

Mr. Sunny got up and stepped back from his castle.

"That's it!" he announced. "*Voilà! Fini!** My sanderpiece is complete!"

"WOW!" everybody said, which is "MOM" upside down.

I spotted Andrea down by the water, so

---

*That's French for "My violin is finished."

me and the guys went over there to pester her. Pestering girls is fun. Especially Andrea. She was eating a piece of pizza and reading one of her Shakespeare books.

"Are you still upset about Mr. Sunny?" I asked her.

"'What's done, is done,'" Andrea said sadly. "'They do not love that do not show their love.' 'Love is a smoke made with the fume of sighs.' 'Fair is foul and foul is fair.'"

I didn't know that Shakespeare guy wrote about baseball.

"Stop moping around," I told Andrea. "You should take my advice and pretend to drown."

"Yeah," said Neil the nude kid, "it's the only way to get Mr. Sunny to notice you."

"And this is the perfect time," Ryan added. "He just finished his sand castle. He's got nothing to do until the judge shows up."

"But what if pretending to drown doesn't work?" Andrea asked, dabbing her eye with a tissue.

"There's only one way to find out," said Michael.

Andrea thought it over. Then she stood up.

"Okay," she said, handing me her book, "I'll do it!"

Andrea went running out into the ocean.

"Don't forget to yell 'help' and 'glub, glub,'" I hollered at her.

"This is gonna be cool," said Ryan.

We all watched as Andrea dived into a wave and swam out into the deep water. That's when the strangest thing in the history of the world happened.

"Shark!" somebody suddenly screamed. "There's a shark out there!"

We all squinted to see. Sure enough, there was a fin moving back and forth. It was on the other side of

the beach from where Andrea was swimming.

"It's probably that crazy guy Mr. Granite," Michael said. "He must be swimming back to Australia."

But it wasn't that crazy guy Mr. Granite. And it wasn't a kid. And it wasn't a lifeguard. And it wasn't my mom or dad or sister. You'll never believe in a million hundred years who it was.

I'm not gonna tell you.

Okay, okay, I'll tell you. But you have to read the next chapter, so nah-nah-nah boo-boo on you!

Glub, Glub

"It's a real, live SHARK!" somebody yelled.

"Eeeeeeeeeeeek!" screamed somebody else.

"Run for your lives!" shouted Neil the nude kid.

Everybody was yelling and screaming

and freaking out. Mr. Sunny blew his whistle and ran down the beach toward the water.

"Leave this to me," he said. "I know how to handle sharks. I'll lure it away from the beach."

"But Mr. Sunny!" I yelled to him. "Andrea—"

"No time for that now!" Mr. Sunny said, and he dived into the water and started swimming toward the shark.

"Help!" yelled Andrea. "I'm drowning!"

"Mr. Sunny can't hear you!" I hollered to Andrea. "He's chasing a shark!"

"Glub, glub," said Andrea.

"Hey, she's pretty good," said Ryan. "She's even doing the 'glub, glub' part."

"Well, she takes acting lessons after school," I told the guys.

"A.J.," said Michael, "I think Andrea might be in trouble."

"Nah, it's all a big act," I told him. "Andrea's a great swimmer. She's been taking swimming lessons since she was three."

Andrea takes lessons in everything. If they gave lessons on how to clean your ears, she would take them so she could get better at it.

"Help!" Andrea yelled. "I have a cramp! Glub, glub."

Then her head went under the water. That's when I realized something.

Andrea wasn't pretending to drown! SHE WAS REALLY DROWNING! And she went swimming right after eating pizza!

The shark might smell the pizza in her stomach and attack her!

Mr. Sunny couldn't hear Andrea's cries for help. He was too busy chasing the shark.

I looked at Michael. Michael looked at Neil. Neil looked at Ryan. Ryan looked at me.

"You should jump in and save her, A.J.," said Ryan.

"Why me?" I asked. "You save her."

"You're the one who's in love with her," Ryan pointed out. "You should save her."

"I am NOT in love with her," I insisted.

"You are too!"

"Am not!"

We went back and forth like that for a while.

"Help!" yelled Andrea.

"There's no time to argue about it!" Neil said. "She's drowning! Are you gonna save her or not?"

"A.J.," Michael said, "if you don't save Andrea, we're gonna tell everybody you're in love with her."

WHAT???!!!

So if I saved Andrea, everybody would think I love her. And if I didn't save Andrea, the guys would tell everybody I love her. No matter what I did, everybody would think I love Andrea.

"Glub, glub," Andrea said. Then she

disappeared under the water.

I didn't know what to do. I didn't know what to say. I had to think fast. I was thinking so hard that my brain hurt.

This was the hardest decision of my life.

A.J. to the Rescue

I ran toward the ocean and jumped into the waves. I swam as fast as I could. Finally, I found Andrea under the water. She was heavy! I picked her up and dragged her back to the beach. She was lying on the sand with her eyes closed.

"Are you okay?" I asked.

Andrea wasn't waking up.

"She can't breathe!" yelled Ryan. "She needs mouth-to-mouth resuscitation!"

"Call Mr. Sunny!" I yelled.

"He's still out there chasing the shark," Michael said.

"You're gonna have to do it, A.J.," said Neil the nude kid.

"Why me?" I asked. "You do it!"

"No, you. "

We went back and forth like that for a while. Andrea was just lying there. Somebody was going to have to do it. So I knelt down next to Andrea and tilted her head back, just like Mr. Sunny showed us. Then I pinched her nostrils shut. Then I leaned over and put my mouth over hers and blew air into it.

Ugh, disgusting! I thought I was gonna die!

"Glub, glub," Andrea said. Then she spit out some water and opened her eyes.

"Oooooh!" Ryan said. "A.J. and Andrea were kissing. They must be in *love*!"

"When are you gonna get married?"

asked Michael.

"Arlo!" Andrea said. "You saved my life! I love you!"

Ewwwwwwwwwwwwwwwwwwwww!

"I thought you were in love with Mr. Sunny," I said, backing away from her as fast as I could.

"That creep?" Andrea said as she

got up. "He's way too old. You're the only man for me, Arlo. 'O, beauty, till now I never knew thee'!"

Andrea was talking that Shakespeare talk and putting her arms all over me.

"Hey, knock it off," I told her.

"O Arlo, Arlo! Wherefore art thou Arlo?"

"Will you leave me alone?" I said, pushing her away. "And quit talking that Shakespeare talk."

"'Good night, sweet prince,'" Andrea said. "'Parting is such sweet sorrow, that I shall say good night till it be morrow.'"

Andrea grabbed me again and leaned over until her mouth was almost touching mine.

She puckered up her lips.

Ewww, disgusting! Andrea was about to kiss me again!

I didn't know what to say! I didn't know what to do! I had to think fast!

"SHARK!" I yelled.

Everybody looked out at the water. In all the excitement over Andrea drowning, we had forgotten about Mr. Sunny!

"Help!" Mr. Sunny yelled. "Help!"

"Did Mr. Sunny take acting lessons?" asked Michael.

"He's drowning, you fobbing, toad-spotted, maggot pie!" said Andrea.

"Oh, snap!" Ryan said. "She called you a fobbing, toad-spotted, maggot pie."

"Help! Help!" called Mr. Sunny as his head dipped below the water. "Glub, glub."

"Mr. Sunny's a lifeguard," said Neil the nude kid. "How can he be drowning?"

"Maybe he's not a real lifeguard," I said. "Did you ever think of that? Maybe he's a fake lifeguard. Maybe he kidnapped our real lifeguard and is holding him in an underground jail cell on a secret island. Stuff like that happens all the time, you know."

But this was not a good time to discuss whether Mr. Sunny was a real lifeguard or not. I ran to the water, jumped in, and swam out to Mr. Sunny. He was even heavier than Andrea! Somehow I managed to drag him to the beach.

"He's not breathing!" Michael said.

"Give him mouth-to-mouth resuscitation, Arlo!" said Ryan.

"Why do I always have to be the one to do it?" I asked.

"He could die, Arlo!" Andrea shouted.

So I knelt down next to Mr. Sunny, tilted his head back, and pinched his nostrils shut. Then I leaned over and put my mouth over his and blew air into it.

Ugh, disgusting! I thought I was gonna die.

"Glub, glub," Mr. Sunny said. Then he spit out some water and opened his eyes. "Thanks, dude! You saved my life."

"Oooooh!" Ryan said. "A.J. and Mr. Sunny were kissing. They must be in *love!*"

"When are you gonna get married?" asked Michael.

"Boys are dumbheads," said Andrea.

And the Winner Is . . .

"Hey, look!" somebody shouted. "The judge for the sand castle contest is coming!"

A guy wearing a tuxedo and one of those tall Abraham Lincoln hats was looking at somebody's sand castle down the beach. He was taking pictures of it and writing on a clipboard. We all ran over to Mr. Sunny.

"This is awesome," I told Mr. Sunny. "You're sure to win the contest, dude."

"I'm glad I put up this fence so nobody could damage my sanderpiece," Mr. Sunny said.

At that moment, the most amazing thing in the history of the world happened.

"Look, up in the sky!" Andrea shouted.

"It's a bird!" Michael shouted.

"It's a plane!" Neil shouted.

"No, it's somebody parasailing!" I shouted.

"It's . . . Mr. Granite!" Ryan shouted.

Sure enough, that crazy, Australian,

long-distance swimming, sand monster
zombie guy was flying through the air

with a parachute on his back. A boat in the water pulled him.

"He's flying pretty low," Andrea said. "I hope he doesn't get hurt."

Mr. Granite flew right over our heads.

"Help! Help!" he shouted. "I can't control this thing!"

Mr. Granite was swooping back and forth, up and down. It looked like he might slam into the beach.

"Watch out!" somebody yelled.

"Run for your lives!" shouted Neil the nude kid.

Suddenly, Mr. Granite started dive-bombing toward the ground.

He was right over our heads!

We dived to get out of the way.

"Oh no!" yelled Mr. Sunny. "He's going to hit–"

Mr. Sunny never got the chance to finish his sentence. Because at that moment Mr. Granite landed right on top of Mr. Sunny's sand castle!

BAM! Mr. Granite crushed it! I mean, it was totally flattened! Mr. Sunny's amazing sand castle looked like a big pile of sand again . . . with a pair of feet sticking out of the top.

"WOW!" everybody said, which is "MOM" upside down.

It was a real Kodak moment. And we got to see it live and in person.

"My sanderpiece is ruined!" Mr. Sunny screamed. "Now I can't go to France to study sand sculpture! My life is over!"

Mr. Sunny went running down the beach, shouting a bunch of French words that I didn't understand. He seemed pretty upset.

I couldn't blame him. I'd be upset too if a shark chased me around and I almost drowned and some nutty parasailor crushed my totally awesome sand castle.

But then, stuff like that happens all the time, you know.

We were standing in front of Mr. Sunny's pile of sand when the judge with the tall Abraham Lincoln hat came over.

"Excuse me," he said, "I heard there is a really amazing sand castle around here. But I don't see it. Can you tell me where it is?"

The Big Surprise Ending That Will Completely Shock You, Unless You Already Guessed It

14

The judge left, and we all helped Mr. Granite crawl out from the pile of sand.

He brushed off his pants.

"Are you okay?" we all asked.

"Yes, I believe I am okay," Mr. Granite said. "I certainly am lucky this sand castle was here to cushion my fall."

"Maybe you better go back to Australia," I told him. "Mr. Sunny is really mad. He might try to beat you up."

"I cannot leave," Mr. Granite said. "I need to stay here for at least a year."

"Why?" Ryan asked.

"I got a job in America, mate," he replied.

"What do you do?" asked Andrea.

"I'm a teacher," Mr. Granite said.

"Oh, really?" asked Andrea. "What grade?"

"I teach third grade," Mr. Granite said.

"Hey, we're going into third grade in September!" Michael said.

"What school will you be teaching at?" asked Neil.

"It has an odd name," Mr. Granite told us. "It's called Ella Mentry School."

WHAT??????!!!!!!!

"That's our school!" I said. "You're going to be our teacher?"

"OH NO!" we all shouted.

Maybe Mr. Granite will be better at teaching than he is at parasailing. Maybe he'll stop popping up in weird places for no reason. Maybe Mr. Sunny will stop talking to sand and learn how to swim. Maybe he'll build a new sand castle. Maybe Andrea will stop talking that Shakespeare talk. Maybe she'll fall in love with some other lifeguard and stop annoying me. Maybe that shark will come back to try and eat Andrea's pizza in her stomach. Maybe people will stop drowning so I won't have to give them mouth-to-mouth resuscitation anymore. Maybe the guys will stop teasing me about being in love with Andrea. Maybe I'll make it through the rest of the summer without any other weird things happening.

But it won't be easy!*

---

*It is a known fact that if you stand up on a chair, put your fingers in your ears, and announce "I love turnips," people will think you're weird.

Read the brand-new My Weird School Daze series starring A.J. and all his wacky teachers!